A Christmas Carol

BY

Charles Dickens

EDITED BY
Philip Page & Marilyn Pettit

ILLUSTRATED BY
Philip Page

LF

Orders: please contact Bookpoint Ltd, 130 Milton Park, Abingdon, Oxon OX14 4SB.
Telephone: (44) 01235 827720, Fax: (44) 01235 400454. Lines are open from 9.00–5.00,
Monday to Saturday, with a 24 hour message answering service.
You can also order through our website: www.hoddereducation.co.uk

British Library Cataloguing in Publication Data
A catalogue record for this title is available from The British Library

ISBN-10: 0 340 78261 7
ISBN-13: 978 0 340 78261 3

First published 2001
Impression number   11
Year   2013

Hodder Headline's policy is to use papers that are natural, renewable and recyclable
products and made from wood grown in sustainable forests. The logging and
manufacturing processes are expected to conform to the environmental regulations of the
country of origin.

Cover illustration by Dave Smith
Typeset by Fakenham Photosetting Ltd, Fakenham, Norfolk
Printed in Great Britain for Hodder Murray, a member of the Hodder
Headline Group, 338 Euston Road, London NW1 3BH by
CPI Group (UK) Ltd, Croydon, CR0 4YY

Contents

About the story

Charles Dickens wrote *A Christmas Carol* in six weeks. It appeared in 1843, just in time for Christmas! He hoped that the book would make him quick money! He also hoped that it would give a message to his readers, one that would teach them a lesson. He cared so much about the conditions in which poor people lived, and the way that children were treated, that he wrote four more Christmas books using the same ideas.

In *A Christmas Carol* there are ghosts, corpses, misery and poverty, but there is also love and hope! Although he used the supernatural in this book, it isn't just a ghost story! It is a novel of protest, one that has a moral.

As you read this story, make a note of the scenes where Dickens shows us hope for the future. Work out what lessons he wants us to learn from his writing. Share your ideas as you read and when you have finished the book.

Characters in the story

Scrooge
A mean and miserly man who cares for no-one.

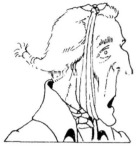

Jacob Marley
Scrooge's dead partner.

Fred
Scrooge's nephew.

Bob Cratchit
Scrooge's poor clerk.

Mrs. Cratchit
Bob's wife.

Tiny Tim
Bob's crippled son

**The Ghost of
Christmas Past**

**The Ghost of
Christmas
Present**

**The Ghost of
Christmas Yet to Come**

The three ghosts who change Scrooge's life.

Scrooge, a mean and miserable man, is introduced to us. We are told that he used to work with a Jacob Marley, but he has died, and now Scrooge is alone.

Marley was dead, to begin with. There is no doubt about that—as dead as a door-nail. Scrooge knew he was dead? Of course he did. Scrooge and he were partners. Scrooge was his **sole** friend, his sole mourner. There is no doubt that Marley was dead. This must be understood, or nothing wonderful can come of the story I am going to **relate**.

sole – only   **relate** – tell

Scrooge was tight-fisted, a squeezing, wrenching, grasping, scraping, clutching, **covetous**, old sinner! The cold within him froze his old features, nipped his pointed nose, shrivelled his cheek, **stiffened his gait**; made his eyes red, his thin lips blue; and spoke out in his grating voice. No warmth could warm, no wintry weather chill him.

Nobody ever stopped him in the street to say, 'How are you? When will you come to see me?' No beggars **implored him to bestow a trifle**, no children asked him what it was o'clock, no man or woman ever once inquired the way to such and such a place, of Scrooge. Even the blind men's dogs appeared to know him; and when they saw him coming, would tug their owners into doorways and up courts.

But what did Scrooge care? It was the very thing he liked.

covetous – greedy   **stiffened his gait** – made him walk stiffly
implored him to bestow a trifle – asked him for a little money

One Christmas Eve, Scrooge has visitors but he treats them all badly! He will not join in and celebrate Christmas. He refuses to give any money to the poor.

Once upon a time—on Christmas Eve—old Scrooge sat busy in his **counting-house**. It was cold. The city clocks had only just gone three, but it was quite dark already. The door of Scrooge's counting-house was open, that he might keep an eye upon his clerk who was copying letters. Scrooge had a very small fire, but the clerk's fire looked like one coal. The clerk tried to warm himself at the candle. He failed.

A merry Christmas uncle!

Bah! **Humbug!**

Christmas a humbug, uncle? You don't mean that, I'm sure.

I do. What reason have you to be merry? You're poor enough.

What right have you to be **dismal**? You're rich enough.

Humbug!

If I could work my will, every idiot who goes about with 'Merry Christmas' on his lips should be boiled with his own pudding and buried with a stake of holly through his heart.

counting-house – office   **Humbug!** – Nonsense!
dismal – miserable

3

Keep Christmas in your way and let me keep it in mine.

But you don't keep it.

Let me leave it alone then.

I have always thought of Christmas as a kind, pleasant time. God bless it!

The clerk applauded.

Another sound from you and you'll keep your Christmas by losing your **situation**!

Don't be angry. Come! Dine with us tomorrow.

Good afternoon.

situation – job

Why cannot we be friends?

Good afternoon.

A Merry Christmas, uncle!

Good afternoon!

And a Happy New Year!

Good afternoon!

4

Two **portly** gentlemen now stood in Scrooge's office.

At this festive season of the year, we should make some provision for the poor.

Are there no prisons?

Plenty.

And **workhouses**?

A few of us are **endeavouring** to raise a fund to buy the Poor some meat and drink and means of warmth. What shall I put you down for?

Nothing! I help to support the establishments I have mentioned. Those who are badly off must go there.

Many would rather die.

They had better do it, and decrease the surplus population. Good afternoon, gentlemen.

portly – fat   **workhouses** – places where the poor lived and worked   **endeavouring** – trying
They had ... population – They should die and cut down the number of people in the country.

The fog and darkness thickened. In the main street some labourers were repairing the gas-pipes, and had lighted a great fire. A party of ragged men and boys were gathered warming their hands.

The brightness of the shops where holly sprigs and berries crackled in the lamp heat of the windows made pale faces **ruddy**.

Scrooge Marley.

God bless you merry gentlemen! May nothing you dismay!

ruddy – red

6

Scrooge is nasty to his clerk, and moans about having to give him Christmas Day off work! After eating, he goes home to his horrible rooms and has some frightening things happen!

The hour of shutting up the counting-house arrived.

You'll want all day tomorrow, I suppose?

If convenient, sir.

It's not convenient when I pay a day's wages for no work. Picking a man's pocket every twenty-fifth of December! Be here all the earlier next morning.

Scrooge took his **melancholy** dinner in his usual melancholy tavern, and went home to bed. He lived in gloomy rooms. The yard was dark. The fog and frost hung about the black old gateway of the house.

melancholy – sad

Scrooge, having his key in the lock of the door, saw in the knocker Marley's face. Though the eyes were wide open, they were motionless. That and its **livid** colour made it horrible.

Scrooge walked in and lighted a candle. He *did* pause, before he shut the door, and he *did* look cautiously behind it first. There was nothing on the back of the door. He fastened the door, and walked across the hall and up the stairs.

Scrooge thought he saw a **hearse** going on before him in the gloom. It was pretty dark. Darkness is cheap, and Scrooge liked it. He walked through all his rooms to see that all was right. Nobody under the table, the sofa, the bed; nobody in the closet.

Satisfied, he closed his door and double-locked himself in.

livid – blue-grey   **hearse** – a carriage for carrying coffins

8

He put on his dressing-gown and slippers and his nightcap and sat down before the fire to take his **gruel**.

The fireplace was old with Dutch tiles.

That face of Marley, seven years dead, came on every one.

Humbug!

His glance happened to rest upon a bell. He saw this bell begin to swing. Soon it rang out loudly, and so did every bell in the house.

gruel – oats and boiled water or milk

The ghost of Jacob Marley, Scrooge's dead partner, visits him. He warns Scrooge that he should be kind or else his spirit will never rest.

The bells ceased. They were **succeeded** by a clanking noise, deep down below as if some person were dragging a heavy chain. The cellar door flew open. He heard the noise much louder on the floors below; then coming up the stairs, then coming straight towards his door.

It's humbug still! I won't believe it!

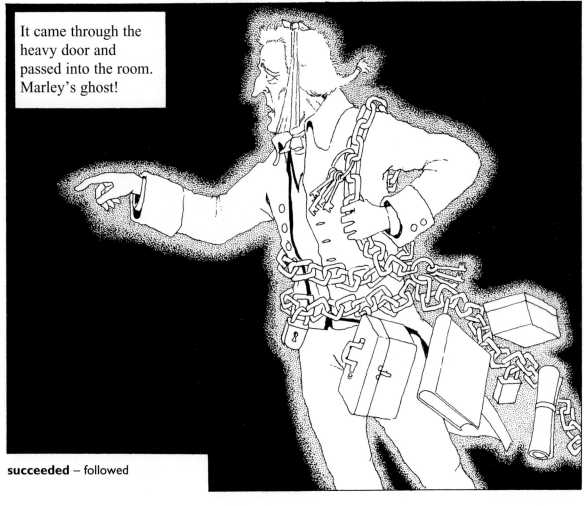

It came through the heavy door and passed into the room. Marley's ghost!

succeeded – followed

Because ... cheats – It's only stomach-ache that makes me imagine you.

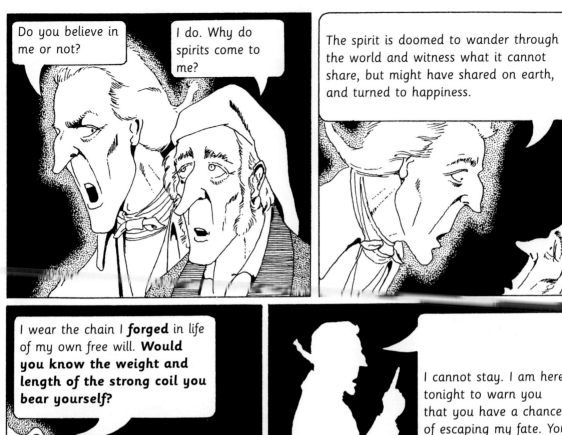

Do you believe in me or not?

I do. Why do spirits come to me?

The spirit is doomed to wander through the world and witness what it cannot share, but might have shared on earth, and turned to happiness.

I wear the chain I **forged** in life of my own free will. **Would you know the weight and length of the strong coil you bear yourself?**

Speak comfort to me, Jacob.

I cannot stay. I am here tonight to warn you that you have a chance of escaping my fate. You will be haunted by three spirits. Expect the first tomorrow when the bell tolls one. Expect the second on the next night at the same hour. The third upon the next night when the last stroke of Twelve has ceased. Remember what has passed between us!

forged – made   **Would you ... bear yourself** – Do you realise how long your chain is?

The window raised itself a little. When the spectre reached it, it was wide open. It beckoned Scrooge to approach. The spectre floated out upon the bleak, dark night.

Scrooge followed to the window.

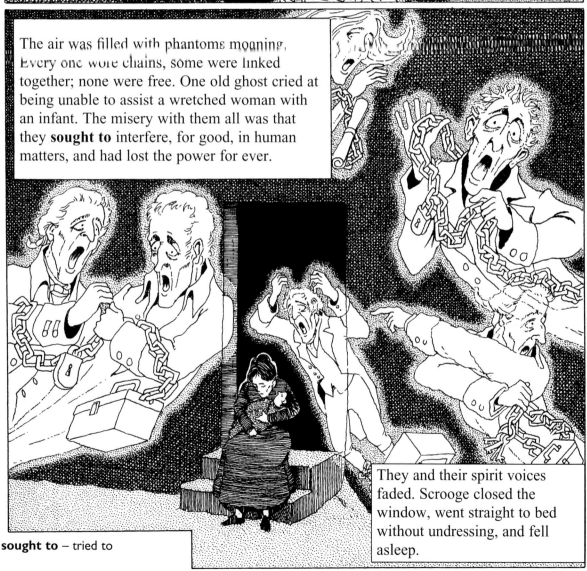

The air was filled with phantoms moaning. Every one wore chains, some were linked together; none were free. One old ghost cried at being unable to assist a wretched woman with an infant. The misery with them all was that they **sought to** interfere, for good, in human matters, and had lost the power for ever.

They and their spirit voices faded. Scrooge closed the window, went straight to bed without undressing, and fell asleep.

sought to – tried to

Time seems to have stopped for Scrooge, but at one o'clock the Ghost of Christmas Past comes to take Scrooge on a journey.

When Scrooge awoke, the chimes of a church struck. He listened. Twelve! It was past two when he went to bed. The clock was wrong.

It isn't possible that I can have slept through a whole day and far into another night.

He groped his way to the window. It was still very foggy and cold. There was no noise of people. This was a great relief.
Scrooge went to bed again, and thought. Marley's Ghost bothered him. Was it a dream or not?

He remembered that the Ghost had warned him of a visitation when the bell tolled one. He **resolved** to lie awake until the hour was passed.

At length the hour bell sounded with a deep, dull, hollow, **melancholy** ONE.

resolved – decided   **melancholy** – sad

14

Lights flashed up. The curtains of his bed were drawn aside. Scrooge found himself face to face with the unearthly visitor. Its hair was white as if with age, yet the face had not a wrinkle. The arms were very long and muscular. Its legs and feet were bare. It wore a tunic of white, and round its waist a belt. It held a branch of fresh green holly: its dress trimmed with summer flowers. From the crown of its head sprang a bright light. Its belt sparkled and glittered.

I am the Ghost of Christmas Past. Your past.

Walk with me!

The Spirit made towards the window.

I am a mortal and liable to fall.

Bear but a touch of my hand there and **you shall be upheld**.

I am . . . to fall – I am human and might fall.   **you . . . upheld** – won't fall

They start their journey at a place where Scrooge was a young boy.

They passed through the wall and stood upon an open country road.

I was a boy here!

They walked along the road. Some ponies were seen trotting towards them with boys upon their backs. Scrooge knew and named them every one. He heard them give each other Merry Christmas. What was merry Christmas to Scrooge? What good had it ever done to him?

The school is not quite deserted. A solitary child, neglected by his friends, is left there still.

Scrooge said he knew it. And he sobbed.

It was a large house. The offices were little used, their walls were damp and mossy, their windows broken, and their gates decayed. They went across the hall to a door. It opened. A lonely boy was reading near a fire.

Scrooge wept to see his poor forgotten self as he used to be.

Poor boy! I wish, but it's too late now.

What is the matter?

There was a boy singing a Carol at my door last night. I should like to have given him something: that's all.

Another Christmas, Scrooge's sister comes to tell him he can come home for good. Scrooge remembers her son is his nephew—the one he treated badly a few hours before, when he visited his counting-house.

Let us see another Christmas.

He was alone again. All the other boys had gone home for the holidays. He was not reading now, but walking up and down. The door opened. A little girl came darting in.

Dear brother. I have come to bring you home!

Father is so much kinder than he used to be, that home's like Heaven! I was not afraid to ask him once more if you might come home; and he said Yes, you should; and sent me in a coach to bring you.

You're never to come back. We're to be together all the Christmas long, and have the merriest time in all the world.

You are quite a woman, little Fan!

She began to drag him towards the door. A terrible voice cried, 'Bring down Master Scrooge's box!' The school-master himself. He **conveyed** him and his sister into the parlour. He produced wine and heavy cake. Master Scrooge's trunk being by this time tied on top of the **chaise**, the children **bade** the school-master goodbye and drove down the garden-sweep.

She had a large heart!

You're right.

She died a woman, and had, as I think, children.

One child.

Your nephew.

Scrooge seemed uneasy.

Yes.

conveyed – took   **chaise** – coach   **bade** – wished

The Ghost takes Scrooge to a place where he once worked. They are all celebrating Christmas.

They were now in a city. It was Christmas time again. The Ghost stopped at a door.

I was apprenticed here!

They went in.

Why, it's old Fezziwig!

Ebenezer! Dick! No more work tonight. Christmas Eve. Let's have the shutters up. Let's have lots of room here!

It was done in a minute. The floor was swept; the lamps were trimmed, fuel was heaped upon the fire. In came a fiddler with a music book. In came Mrs Fezziwig, three Miss Fezziwigs, young men and women, the housemaid, the baker, the milkman. In they all came. Old Fezziwig, clapping his hands, cried out, 'Well done!'

There were more dances, and there was cake, **negus**, a great piece of Cold Roast, a great piece of Cold Boiled, mincepies, and plenty of beer. Then old Fezziwig stood out to dance with Mrs Fezziwig.

When the clock struck eleven this ball broke up. The lads were left to their beds pouring out their hearts in praise of Fezziwig.

He has spent a few pounds of your mortal money. Is that so much that he deserves this praise?

It isn't that, Spirit. He has the power to **render** us happy or unhappy. The happiness he gives is quite as great as if it cost a fortune.

What is the matter? Something, I think?

No, I should like to be able to say a word or two to my clerk just now. That's all.

negus – spiced wine   **render** – make

21

Scrooge sees the girl who loved him once. She left him, because his greed for money spoilt their relationship.

My time grows short. Quick!

Again Scrooge saw himself, sat by the side of a fair young girl, in whose eyes there were tears.

It matters little to you. Another idol has displaced me.

What idol?

A golden one. **Gain engrossed you**.

I am not changed towards you. Am I?

You are changed. If you were free today, tomorrow, yesterday, can I believe that you would choose a **dowerless girl**—you, who weighs everything by Gain? I release you. May you be happy in the life you have chosen.

Show me no more! Why do you torture me?

Gain engrossed you – You only think of money.   **dowerless girl** – a girl with no money

Scrooge is taken to see this same girl—the one who once loved him. She has a very happy family now. Her husband tells her he has seen Scrooge—alone! Scrooge cannot stand seeing all this.

They were in another place. Near the winter fire sat a beautiful young girl so like that last that Scrooge believed it was the same until he saw HER sitting opposite her daughter. There were more children. The mother and daughter laughed. The father came home attended by a man laden with Christmas toys and presents. The shouts of wonder and delight!

The children went to bed.

I saw an old friend of yours this afternoon.

Who was it?

Mr Scrooge. He sat alone, quite alone in the world.

Remove me from this place!

They are what they are, do not blame me!

I cannot bear it! Take me back!

He was conscious of being in his own bedroom. He sank into a heavy sleep.

Scrooge meets the Ghost of Christmas Present!

The bell was again on the stroke of One. No shape appeared. Five minutes, ten minutes, a quarter of an hour went by, yet nothing came. Scrooge lay in his bed the centre of a blaze of light. He began to think that this ghostly light might be in the **adjoining room**. He got up and shuffled in his slippers to the door.

A strange voice called him and bade him enter.

It was his own room. The walls and ceiling were hung with green holly, mistletoe and ivy. A mighty blaze went roaring up the chimney. Heaped upon the floor were turkeys, geese, game, poultry, brawn, great joints of meat, sucking-pigs, sausages, mince pies, plum puddings, barrels of oysters, red hot chestnuts, cherry cheeked apples, juicy oranges, pears, cake and bowls of punch.

Come in! I am the Ghost of Christmas Present!

adjoining room – room next door

24

The Ghost takes Scrooge on a journey through London.

Spirit, if you have **aught** to teach me, let me profit by it.

Touch my robe!

They stood in the city on Christmas morning. There was nothing cheerful and yet there was an air of cheerfulness. The people who were shovelling away were calling out to one another exchanging a snowball. The shops were still open. Baskets of chestnuts, Spanish onions, pears and apples, grapes, oranges and lemons to be carried home and eaten after dinner.

The Grocers! The scent of tea and coffee! Customers were so hurried that they tumbled up against each other at the door, left their purchases upon the counter, and came running back to fetch them.

But soon the steeples called good people to church in their best clothes.

aught – anything

Scrooge and the Spirit arrive at Bob Cratchit's house. Bob works for Scrooge as his clerk. Scrooge sees the happy family life Bob has and learns something about himself – but it isn't very nice!

The Spirit stopped to bless Bob Cratchit's dwelling. Mrs Cratchit laid the cloth, assisted by Belinda; Peter Cratchit plunged a fork into the saucepan of potatoes; two smaller Cratchits, boy and girl, came tearing in, screaming that outside the baker's they had smelt the goose.

What has got your father then? And Tiny Tim? And Martha warn't as late last Christmas.

We'd a deal of work to finish up last night and had to clear away this morning, mother!

Here's Martha, mother. There's such a goose, Martha!

Never mind. Sit down and have a warm.

There's father coming!

In came Bob, Tiny Tim upon his shoulder.

How did Tim behave?

As good as gold. He hoped the people saw him in church, because he was a cripple, and it might be pleasant to them to remember who made lame beggars walk and blind men see.

Bob **compounded** some hot mixture in a jug with gin and lemons, and put it on the hob to simmer. Peter, and the two young Cratchits, **went to fetch the goose**. Mrs Cratchit made the gravy, Peter mashed the potatoes, Belinda sweetened the apple-sauce. Bob said he didn't believe there ever was such a goose cooked.

Everyone had had enough. But now Mrs Cratchit left the room to take the pudding up and bring it in.

compounded – mixed   **went to fetch the goose** – from the baker's who had cooked it for them

At last the dinner was all done. The compound in the jug being tasted, and considered perfect, apples and oranges were put upon the table, and a shovel-full of chestnuts on the fire. The Cratchit family drew round the hearth.

A Merry Christmas to us all, my dears.

God bless us every one!

Spirit, tell me if Tiny Tim will live.

I see a vacant seat in the poor chimney-corner, and a crutch without an owner.

No, no! say he will be spared.

If he be like to die, he had better do it, and decrease the surplus population.

Scrooge hung his head to hear his own words.

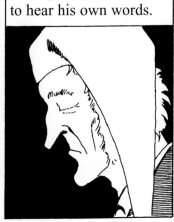

Will you decide what men shall live, what men shall die?

Scrooge cast his eyes upon the ground, but he raised them on hearing his name.

I'll give you Mr Scrooge.

I wish I had him here. I'd give him a piece of my mind to feast upon.

My dear! The children! Christmas Day!

It should be Christmas Day on which one drinks the health of such an **odious, stingy**, hard, unfeeling man as Mr Scrooge. You know he is Robert! I'll drink his health for your sake and the day's, not for his.

Scrooge was the Ogre of the family. His name cast a dark shadow on the party. After it had passed away, they were ten times merrier than before. The chestnuts and the jug went round and round and they had a song about a lost child in the snow from Tiny Tim.

They were not a handsome family, not well dressed; but they were happy with one another and when they faded, Scrooge had his eye on them especially Tiny Tim.

odious – horrible   **stingy** – mean

Scrooge and the Ghost visit lots of places where people are enjoying themselves, even though they have hard lives and very little money.

It was getting dark, and snowing heavily. Scrooge and the Spirit went along the streets. Here the flickering of the blaze showed preparations for a cosy dinner. There the children of the house were running out into the snow to meet their sisters, brothers, cousins, uncles, aunts.

And now they stood upon a bleak moor. Nothing grew but moss and **furze** and coarse grass.

What place is this?

A place where Miners live.

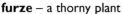
furze – a thorny plant

A light shone from the window of a hut. Passing through the wall of mud and stone, they found a cheerful company. The old man was singing a Christmas song.

The Spirit did not **tarry** here but sped to sea.

Two men wished each other Merry Christmas.

The Ghost sped on.

They **lighted** on a ship.

Every man hummed a Christmas tune. Every man had a kinder word for another that day, and had remembered those he cared for at a distance.

tarry – stay long   lighted – landed

Scrooge sees his nephew and once again, he hears what others think of him—and it still isn't very nice!

It was a great surprise to Scrooge to hear a laugh. It was a much greater surprise to Scrooge to recognise his own nephew.

He said that Christmas was a humbug!

More shame for him, Fred!

He's a comical old fellow and not so pleasant as he might be. However, **his offences carry their own punishment**. I have nothing to say against him.

I'm sure he's very rich, Fred.

His wealth is of no use to him. He don't do any good with it. He don't make himself comfortable with it.

I have no patience with him.

I have. I am sorry for him. Who suffers by his ill whims? Himself, always!

Do go on, Fred.

I was only going to say he loses some pleasant moments. I mean to give him the same chance every year. I pity him. I think I **shook him** yesterday.

his offences ... punishment – only he suffers   **shook him** – made him think

After tea they had some music.
Scrooge softened more and more.

They played forfeits,
blind man's buff,
How, When and
Where. They all
played and so did
Scrooge forgetting that
his noise made no
sound in their ears.

Here is a new game.

A game called Yes and
No. Scrooge's nephew
had to think of
something and the rest
must find out what.
The questioning
elicited from him that
he was thinking of a
disagreeable animal
that growled and
grunted sometimes,
and lived in London,
and walked the streets.

I know what it is! It's
your Uncle Scro-o-o-o-
oge!

Which it was.

It would be
ungrateful not to
drink his health.

A Merry Christmas
and a Happy New
Year to the old man,
whatever he is!

elicited – got

At last their journey is over. Scrooge has just one shock left, when he looks at the young children who are huddled near the Ghost.

He and the Spirit were again upon their travels. In almshouse, hospital, jail, the Spirit left his blessing.

It was strange. The Ghost grew older. Its hair was grey.

Are spirits' lives so short?

My life ends tonight at midnight.

I see something strange. Is it a foot or a claw?

From its robe it brought out two children, hideous, miserable.

Are they yours?

They are Man's. This boy is Ignorance. This girl is Want. Beware them both.

Have they no refuge or resource?

Are there no prisons? Are there no work-houses?

The bell struck twelve.

Scrooge looked about him for the Ghost and saw it not.

The Ghost of the Future shows Scrooge what people will think of him when he dies—that is, if he doesn't change his ways!

He remembered the prediction of old Jacob Marley, and lifting up his eyes, beheld a Phantom coming like a mist along the ground towards him.

I am in the presence of the Ghost of Christmas Yet To Come?

Ghost of the Future! I fear you more than any other spectre I have seen. But as I know your purpose is to do me good, and as I hope to live to be another man from what I was, I am prepared to bear your company, and do it with a thankful heart. Will you not speak to me?

Lead on!

A group of men are talking about someone who has just died.

The Phantom glided on into a street. Its finger pointed to two persons meeting. Scrooge listened.

Old Scratch has got his own at last, hey?

So I am told. Cold, isn't it?

Scrooge was surprised that the spirit attached importance to conversations so **trivial. They could scarcely have any bearing on the death of Jacob**, his old partner. This Ghost was the Future. Nor could he think of anyone immediately connected with himself to whom he could apply them.

He fancied the Unseen Eyes were looking at him. It made him shudder.

Old Scratch – the Devil   **trivial** – silly/unimportant
They could ... of Jacob – They couldn't have anything to do with Jacob's death.

They move on to a shop, where some people are selling goods that they have taken from the dead man's place.

They left the busy scene, and went to an **obscure part** of the town. The ways were foul and narrow; the shops and houses wretched; the people half-naked, drunken, ugly. The whole quarter reeked with crime, filth and misery.

There was a shop where iron, old rags, bottles, bones and greasy **offal** were bought.

Let the charwoman be first. The laundress second; the undertaker's man third.

Come into the parlour.

The woman threw her bundle on the floor.

Every person has a right to take care of themselves. He always did.

If he wanted to keep 'em after he was dead why wasn't he more natural in his lifetime? If he had been, he'd have had somebody to look after him when he was struck with Death, instead of lying gasping out his last there, alone by himself.

obscure part – an area that was not well known   **offal** – rubbish

39

It's a judgement on him.

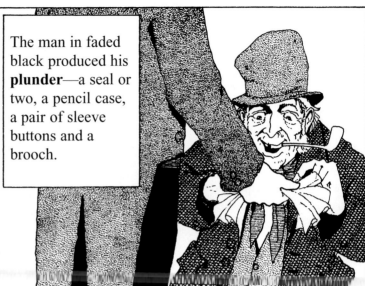

The man in faded black produced his **plunder**—a seal or two, a pencil case, a pair of sleeve buttons and a brooch.

Mrs Dilber was next. Sheets, towels, **a little wearing apparel**, two old fashioned silver teaspoons, a pair of sugar tongs and a few boots.

Undo my bundle.

What do you call this? Bed curtains! His blankets! I hope he didn't die of anything catching?

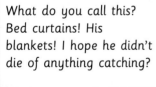

You won't find a hole in it. They'd have wasted it – putting it on him to be buried in!

Spirit! The case of this unhappy man might be my own.

plunder – stolen goods **a little wearing apparel** – a few clothes

Scrooge visits the room where the dead man lies on the bed. The body and face are covered. Scrooge is too scared to look and find out who it is.

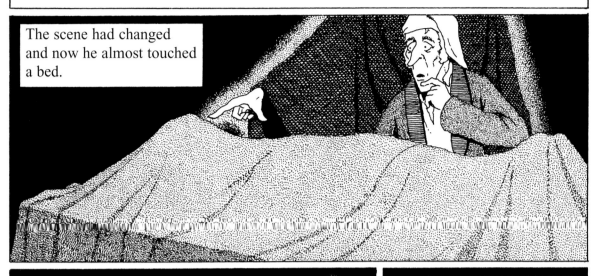

The scene had changed and now he almost touched a bed.

A cat was tearing at the door and there was a sound of gnawing rats. What they wanted in the room of death, Scrooge did not dare to think.

Let us go!

I would do it, if I could. But I have not the power.

Scrooge wants to know if anyone cares about the man who has died.

If there is any person in the town who feels emotion caused by this man's death, show that person to me.

A room by daylight; a mother and her children. The long expected knock was heard. She hurried to the door, and met her husband. She asked him faintly what news.

Is it good or bad?

Bad.

There is hope yet, Caroline. He is dead.

She was thankful to hear it and she said so. She prayed forgiveness the next moment.

When I tried to see him and obtain a week's delay he was not only very ill but dying.

To whom will our debt be transferred?

I don't know. But before that time we shall be ready with the money. We may sleep tonight with light hearts.

Yes. The only emotion that the Ghost could show him was one of pleasure.

To whom ... transferred? – Who will we owe the money to now?

They move on to the Cratchits' house and hear some sad news about Tiny Tim.

Let me see some tenderness connected with a death.

They entered poor Bob Cratchit's house.

Quiet. Very quiet.

His father loved him so. And there is your father at the door.

You went today then, Robert?

Yes my dear. I wish you could have gone. It would have done you good to see how green a place it is. But you'll see it often. I promised him that I would walk there on a Sunday.

My little child!

Bob told them of the kindness of Mr Scrooge's nephew.

'If I can be of service to you in any way,' he said, giving me his card, 'that's where I live. Pray come to me.'

I'm sure he's a good soul.

I am sure we shall none of us forget Tiny Tim.

No, never, father!

At last Scrooge finds out who the dead man is. He visits his office but can't see himself working there. Then ... in a churchyard, he reads a name on the gravestone.

Tell me what man that was whom we saw lying dead?

This is where my place of occupation is. Let me **behold** what I shall be in days to come.

The house is **yonder**. Why do you point away?

Scrooge hastened to the window of his office, and looked in. It was an office still, but not his. The figure in the chair was not himself.

behold – see   **yonder** – over there

The Phantom pointed as before. He joined it once again.

They reached an iron gate. He paused to look round before entering.

A churchyard. Walled in by houses; overrun by grass and weeds; choked up with too much burying.

The Spirit stood among the graves, and pointed down to one.

Before I draw nearer to that stone to which you point, answer me one question. Are these shadows of the things that Will be, or are they shadows of the things that May be, only?

Still the Ghost pointed downward to the grave.

Scrooge crept towards it, trembling as he went.

Am I that man who lay upon the bed? No, Spirit! Oh, no, no!

Spirit! Hear me! I am not the man I was. Why show me this, if I am past all hope?

Assure me that I yet may change these shadows you have shown me. I will honour Christmas in my heart and try to keep it all the year. I will not shut out the lessons that they teach. Tell me I may sponge away the writing on this stone!

The hand trembled.

The Phantom shrunk, collapsed, and dwindled down into a bedpost.

Scrooge has changed! He has learnt his lesson and begins to do good for others.

And the bedpost was his own.

I don't know what day of the month it is! I don't know anything! Never mind. I don't care.

Running to the window, he opened it, and put out his head. No fog, no mist.

What's today?

Today! Why, Christmas Day.

I haven't missed it. The Spirits have done it all in one night.

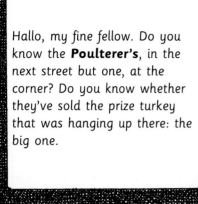

Hallo, my fine fellow. Do you know the **Poulterer's**, in the next street but one, at the corner? Do you know whether they've sold the prize turkey that was hanging up there: the big one.

What, the one as big as me?

It's hanging there now.

Go and buy it. Tell 'em to bring it here. Come back with the man, and I'll give you a shilling. Come back with him in less than five minutes and I'll give you half a crown!

The boy was off like a shot.

I'll send it to Bob Cratchit's. He shan't know who sends it.

He wrote the address and went downstairs to open the street door, ready for the poulterer's man.

It's impossible to carry that to Camden Town. You must have a cab!

Poulterer's – butcher's

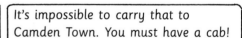

50

He sat down and chuckled till he cried.

Shaving was not an easy task, for his hand continued to shake.

He dressed himself all in his best, and at last got out into the streets.

He had not gone far, when coming towards him he beheld the portly gentleman, who had walked into his counting-house the day before.

My dear sir, I hope you succeeded yesterday?

Mr Scrooge?

Yes. Allow me to ask your pardon. And will you have the goodness—

Mr Scrooge, are you serious?

A great many back payments are included.

I don't know what to say!

Don't say anything please. Will you come and see me?

I will.

He went to church, and walked about the streets, and patted children on the head, questioned beggars, looked down into kitchens of houses. He never dreamed any walk could give him so much happiness.

In the afternoon he turned his steps towards his nephew's house.

Is your master at home, my dear?

Yes, sir.

He knows me. I'll go in here.

His last good turn is to Bob Cratchit and his family.

He was early at the office next morning.

Scrooge & Marley

The clock struck nine. No Bob. A quarter past. No Bob.

He was a full eighteen minutes and a half behind his time.

What do you mean by coming here at this time of day?

I am very sorry sir. I am behind my time.

E. Scrooge

A merry Christmas, Bob!

I'll raise your salary and **endeavour** to assist your struggling family.

endeavour – try

Make up the fires and buy another coal scuttle before you dot another 'i', Bob Cratchit!

Scrooge did it all, and to Tiny Tim, who did NOT die, he was a second father. Some people laughed to see the alteration in him but he let them laugh. His own heart laughed and that was quite enough for him.

It was always said that he knew how to keep Christmas well. May that be truly said of all of us! And so, as Tiny Tim observed, God bless Us, Every One!

THE END